KITCHEN FUN

**By the editors of
OWL and *Chickadee* Magazines**

Edited by Catherine Ripley

Joy Street Books
Little, Brown and Company
Boston   Toronto   London

First U.S. edition

Special thanks to Sylvia Funston, editor of *OWL* Magazine, and Janis Nostbakken, editor of *Chickadee* Magazine, and to all those people who worked with them on creating most of the ideas and images found in this book: Marilyn Baillie, Lina di Nardo, Laima Dingwall, Katherine Grier, Nancy Harvey, Michele Kraft, Elizabeth MacLeod, Jonathan Milne, Nick Milton, Gordon Penrose, Laurie Peters, Cathy Ripley, Wycliffe Smith and Valerie Wyatt.

Photography: Ray Boudreau (Cover, pages 5, 6–7, 8–9, 14, 16–17, 18, 21, 23, 26–27, 29, 31), Nigel Dickson (pages 11, 29), Hal Roth (pages 26–27), Tony Thomas (pages 10, 13, 15, 19, 22, 25) and Ron Watts (Page 7).

Illustration: Anita Granger (page 12, 32), Joe Weissmann (page 4)

Design: Wycliffe Smith

First published in Canada in 1988 by
Greey de Pencier Books,
56 The Esplanade, Suite 306,
Toronto, Ontario,
M5E 1A7, Canada.

Library of Congress Catalog Card Number 88–82303

Joy Street Books are published
by Little, Brown and Company (Inc.)

PRINTED IN SINGAPORE

Contents

Wacky Walnuts

Save those walnut shells!
They turn into fabulous fridge magnets
and make great gifts, too.

You'll Need:

Cleaned-out walnut halves (*Ask an adult to slide a screwdriver down the middle of the nuts to split them.*)
Poster paint
Clear nail polish
White glue
Scissors
Decorating materials (pasta, pipe cleaners, colored paper...)
Felt or construction paper
Magnetic tape (found in craft stores)

Here's How:

■ Paint the shells. When dry, put on a coat of clear nail polish.
■ Add eyes, ears, whiskers, or tails with your decorating materials.

■ Cut a piece of felt to fit the bottom of the shell and glue in place.
■ Now paste a piece of magnetic tape to the felt, and your fridge magnet is ready to stick up.

Fortune Nuts

Make a bunch of fortune nuts for your friends and see who chooses which future. Ask an adult to split the walnuts down the middle with a screwdriver. Clean out the nut meat. Then pop in fortunes written on strips of paper. Stick the walnuts back together using white glue.

Leftover Art

at do
call a
nut
sticks
the
dge ?

A
magNUT,
of course !!

Peanut Puppets

Don't throw out those peanut
shells just yet! They can turn into
great puppets. Put a funny face
on each half with a marker, and
pop them on your fingers. Then let
your fingers do the talking!

Bird
Eggs-travaganza

Wait! Don't crack that egg!
Instead blow the inside out, save the shell,
and transform it into a very
"tweet" bird.

You'll Need:

Raw eggs
Pin or thick needle
Bowls
Food coloring
Decorating materials (markers,
    paints, pipe cleaners,
    construction paper...)
Brightly colored embroidery
    thread or wool

Here's How:

■ Ask an adult to help you tap
the pin into the small end of an
egg.
■ Now make a bigger hole in the
other end.
■ Blow through the small hole
and watch the insides come out
the other end into a bowl.

■ When you've blown several
eggs, scramble up the insides for
a meal.
■ Wash the shells carefully and
dry.

■ Dip the eggs in bowls of food
coloring mixed with water and let
them sit for a few minutes.
■ Remove and let dry.

■ Place each egg on its side and
start adding bird decorations
(construction paper wings and
beak, marker or split-pea eyes,
pipe-cleaner feet).
■ Thread the wool through the
small hole with a long needle and
pull through the other end. Tie a
knot to complete your hanging
loop.
■ Hang the birdies from twigs in
a table vase or let them fly from a
mobile. How tweet!

Who lays the largest egg in the world?

**An ostrich! One ostrich
egg weighs as much as
two dozen chicken
eggs.**

Build with Bones

This dinosaur looks as though it belongs in a museum,
but it's made from chicken bones!

You'll Need:

Chicken carcass
Pot filled with water

Cookie sheet
White glue
Modeling clay
Heavy paper

Leftover Art

Here's How:

(Ask an adult for help.)

■ Boil the bones for 30 minutes.
■ When the bones are cool enough to touch, scrape the bones clean. The leftover chicken meat and water are a good start for homemade soup.

■ Bake the bones in the oven at a low temperature for 30 minutes.
■ Now design a dinosaur. White glue works best for sticking the bones on paper, and modeling clay holds the bones together well.
■ The bird's breastbone makes a perfect pterodactyl, one of the huge flying reptiles from dinosaur days.

Kitchen Challenge 1.

How can you make a chicken bone bend?

See page 32 for the answer.

Ta Da!

Amaze your friends with some everyday magic.
All you need are a few things from your kitchen cupboards.

SPOON TRICK

Test your sense of balance by doing this spoon trick.

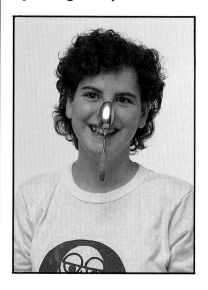

Here's How:

■ Hold the spoon with the handle down.
■ Place the bowl over the tip of your nose.
■ When you sense that the spoon is balancing by itself, let go. Ta da!

Why?

Just like the spoon, every object has a balancing point. What else can you balance on your body?

KNIFE TRICK

Pick up a heavy jar of rice with only a knife.

Here's How:

(Ask an adult for help.)

■ Work over a table or counter at all times while doing this trick.
■ Fill a narrow-necked jar with uncooked rice.
■ Jab a serrated or plain steel knife about 1 inch into the rice over and over again for a minute.
■ Now plunge the knife deep into the rice and lift carefully. Ta da!

Why?

Friction is strong! It is the friction between the tightly packed rice and the knife that lets you lift the jar.

WATER TRICK

How can you float a cork in a glass of water so it doesn't touch the sides?

Here's How:

■ Slowly fill a glass with water so the top bulges up into a dome.
■ Place the cork in the middle of the dome. Ta da!

Why?

The cork is lighter than the water so it floats at the highest point of the water dome. What else will float here?

Kitchen Challenge 2.

How can you make a single sheet of paper hold up a heavy cookbook?

See page 32 for the answer.

Presto!

Volcano Countdown

Make a volcano erupt on your very own kitchen table.

You'll Need:

Empty flower pot placed upside down in a large, deep baking pan

Empty tuna tin with one end removed

Plastic or paper cup with the bottom cut off, upside down on the tin (*Pull the sides of the cup together tightly around the tin and tape. You may have to cut a small v in the side of the cup to make it fit snugly.*)

Scissors

Masking tape

Tinfoil

Spoons

½ cup vinegar

Baking soda

Red food coloring or powdered paint

Dishwashing detergent

Here's How:

■ Put the tin and paper cup on top of the flower pot.

■ Cover your "mountain" with tinfoil and crinkle it.

■ Cut an X on top of the foil and fold it down inside the cup to make a hole.

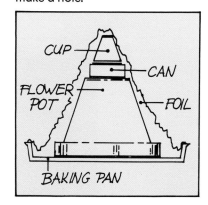

■ Add a spoonful of baking soda and a spoonful of dishwashing detergent to the tin through the hole.

■ Measure out the vinegar and add a spoonful of food coloring.

■ Start your volcano countdown as you pour the vinegar through the hole. Presto!

Volcanoes even erupt underwater!

Deep-sea volcanoes are mountain makers, and in places, island makers. Iceland is one island that was made by volcanoes. Watch for the next volcano to rise from the depths of the sea. It's scheduled to appear in the Caribbean in the year 2000 and will be called Kick'em Jenny.

Presto!

Incredible Cookies

Make three amazing types of cookies— all from one basic recipe.

You'll Need:

1 cup brown sugar,
    ¹/₂ cup margarine,
    1 egg, 1 tsp vanilla
    (*Beat these ingredients
    together first.*)
1¹/₄ cup flour,
    ¹/₂ tsp baking powder,
    ¹/₂ tsp salt
    (*Mix these ingredients
    together and then add to
    the margarine mixture.*)
Mixing bowls, spoons, greased
    cookie sheets
Preheated oven
(*Ask an adult for help.*)

RAINBOW GLASS COOKIES

Extra ingredients: about 1 cup
    extra flour, tinfoil, smashed
    clear candies (*Ask an adult to
    help you smash them, one
    color at a time, with a hammer
    between waxed paper.*)
Oven temperature: 325°F

■ Add the extra flour until the dough feels like soft clay. If it's too dry, add a little water.
■ Chill the dough for 20 minutes in the freezer.
■ Roll out dough snakes on a flat surface.
■ Make designs with the snakes on a foil-lined cookie sheet. Press the ends of each shape together with your fingers.
■ Bake the cookies for about 5 minutes—don't let them brown!
■ Ask an adult to help you take the cookies out of the oven.
■ Fill each shape with an even layer of smashed candies. Watch out—the pan will be hot.

■ Put them back in the oven. In about 5 minutes, the candy will start to bubble. Remove the pan.
■ Cool the cookies for about 30 minutes. Then pull the foil off the back of the cookies. Hang them in a cool place for decoration or eat them. Mmmm!

Which bitter beans turn into a sweet and scrumptious treat?

Cocoa beans, of course! They grow in the hottest part of the world. Before they get to you in your local store as chocolate, they are picked, fermented, dried, roasted, crushed, cooled, pressed, kneaded, heated, and again cooled!

Digging into Dough

COOKIE POPS

Extra ingredients: chocolate chips, wooden ice cream sticks, food coloring (optional), waxed paper
Oven temperature: 400°F

■ Wrap the dough mixture in waxed paper and refrigerate one hour.
■ Make thin dough sandwiches with chocolate chips inside and seal the edges.

■ Push a wooden stick into each one and bake on a cookie sheet for 8 minutes.
■ Be sure to let the pops cool completely before lifting off the cookie sheet.

Smile!
Did you know that chocolate causes certain glands in your body to secrete hormones that can make you feel happier?

GIFT BOX

Extra ingredients: ³/₄ cup chocolate chips, a greased tinfoil pattern scaled up from the one given below
Oven temperature: 350°F

■ Add ¹/₂ cup of the chocolate chips to your dough mixture.

■ Carefully pat out the dough to fill the tinfoil shapes, until it is about ³/₈ inch thick.

Scale these up to whatever size you like

Top	Side	Bot.	Ends
cut 1	cut 2	cut 1	cut 2

■ Place the shapes on a cookie sheet and bake in the oven for about 10 minutes.
■ Ask an adult to help you melt the rest of the chocolate chips over hot water.
■ Glue your box together with the melted chocolate and support the sides until the "glue" sets.

Pass the Pizza

What's this? Tiny fish pizzas? Don't stop there —
What about face pizzas? Stop sign pizzas? Even house pizzas?
The sky's the limit!

You'll Need:

2 cups flour, 2 tsp baking powder, 1/2 tsp salt (*Mix together in a bowl.*)

1/4 cup olive oil, 1/4 cup milk, 2 eggs (*Mix together, add to dry ingredients and stir until dough is stiff.*)

Spaghetti sauce

Your favorite pizza toppings (pepperoni, green pepper, pineapple, mushrooms, olives...)

Bowls, wooden spoon, rolling pin, greased cookie sheet

Oven preheated to 375°F (*Ask an adult to help.*)

Here's How:

■ When all of the flour has disappeared in the dough mixture, put it out on a counter sprinkled with flour.

■ Rub flour on the rolling pin and roll the dough out until it's 1/4 inch thick.

■ Shape and cut the dough into any shape you want and then carefully place it on the cookie sheet.

■ Spoon on a thin layer of the spaghetti sauce.

■ Add the toppings to complete your design.

■ Bake the pizzas—about 18 minutes for smaller ones or 25 minutes for one large one.

Who invented pizza?

The Greeks did—almost three thousand years ago! The first pizzas were simple, made from local flour, olive oil, olives, herbs, and cheeses. It wasn't until the 1800s that the rest of the world began to catch on to the idea of pizza, the perfect plate—one you eat instead of wash!

Digging into Dough

Sourdough Surprise

Here's a cake with a pioneering heart! It's based on a yeast starter that has been passed down to us from the early settlers of North America.

START SOME STARTER

You'll Need:

2 cups warm water
1 pkg. active dry yeast
1 tbsp sugar
2 cups all-purpose flour
Glass bowl
Wooden spoon
Clean cloth

Here's How:

■ Mix up the starter ingredients.
■ Cover with the cloth and place in a warm, draft-free place for about 6 hours.

■ Store the starter in a plastic container in the fridge until ready to make your cake or give some away.

■ If you want to share your starter with friends, give them plastic containers with the starter inside and tags that read: Store me in the fridge and feed me equal amounts of water and flour every 7-10 days. After you feed me, let me stand at room temperature overnight. Then use some of me to make a sourdough cake and pass on the rest.

Listen! Can you hear the starter growing?

The yeast in the starter is a type of fungus that multiplies quickly when given warm water and sugar to feed on. As the yeast grows, it produces noisy bubbles of carbon dioxide.

Digging into Dough

SOURDOUGH CHOCOLATE CAKE

You'll Need:

1 cup margarine, 2 cups sugar, 2 eggs, 1 tsp vanilla, 1 cup sourdough starter, 1/3 cup milk (*Blend ingredients together in the order listed.*)

2 cups all-purpose flour, 1 tsp baking soda, 2/3 cup unsweetened cocoa (*Mix together well.*)
Icing
Mixing bowls, measuring cups, spoons
8 inch greased round cake pan
8 inch greased square cake pan
Oven preheated to 350°F (*Ask an adult.*)

Here's How:

■ Add the dry ingredients to the ''wet'' ones and stir well.
■ Pour half the batter into each pan and bake for 30-40 minutes.
■ Cool the cakes on racks.
■ Then cut and assemble the cakes as shown in the pattern.
■ Ice with your favorite icing.

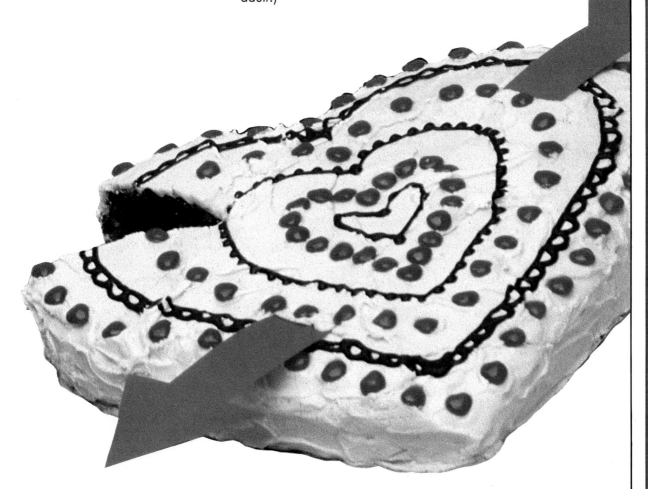

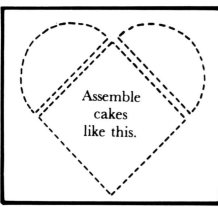

Assemble cakes like this.

Perfect Pretzels

If your lunches are ho-hum, pack a homemade pretzel into your brown bag for a change of pace!

You'll Need:

1 cup warm water,
   1 tbsp dry yeast,
   1 tbsp honey (*Mix together in a bowl, set it in a warm place for 10 minutes or until yeast is bubbling.*)
1 tbsp oil
1 tsp salt
1 cup whole wheat flour
2½ cups all-purpose flour
Egg white
Mixing bowl, measuring cup and spoons, clean damp cloth, wooden spoon, rolling pin, knife, cookie sheet

Here's How:

■ Stir the oil and salt into the yeast mixture, and little by little, add the flour.

■ When the dough is too stiff to stir, put it on a floured counter.

■ Knead it well by punching the middle of the dough and folding in the sides.

■ Punch and fold for about 10 minutes or until the dough is smooth and stretchy.

■ Put the dough into a clean, greased bowl, cover it with the cloth, and place in a warm place for an hour.

■ When the dough has risen to twice its original size, you can start pretzelling.

■ First ask an adult to preheat the oven to 400°F.

■ Roll out the dough on a clean surface until it is ½ inch thick and cut into thin strips.

■ Make dough snakes and shape into letters or animals or whatever you like.

■ Place the shapes on a cookie sheet and paint with egg white.

■ Bake until golden brown, about 8-10 minutes.

Kitchen Challenge 3.

How can a pretzel turn iodine from red to black?

Turn to page 32 for the answer.

Digging into Dough

Ice is Nice

Use your freezer to transform juice and water to super ice surprises. MMMMM good!

ICE PUPPETS

Make some neat ice puppets and then slurp them up for a cool treat.

You'll Need:

Plastic baby food containers or
    yogurt containers
Wooden ice cream sticks
Icing paste (*Drip cold water
    slowly into 2 tbsp icing sugar
    until thick and sticky*.)
Face decorations (raisins, orange
    pieces, chocolate chips,
    assorted berries…)
Skirts (tinfoil or cloth squares)
Paper towels or napkins

Here's How:

■ Dip your finger in the icing paste and draw a face on the inside of the container. Then press the face decorations firmly into place in the icing paste. (See illustration 1.)
■ Secure the wooden stick to the bottom of the container with a big blob of icing paste. (See illustration 2.) Freeze container for about ½ hour or until icing is frozen.
■ Remove from freezer and fill the container with your favorite juice. Put container back into freezer for a couple of hours, or until frozen.

■ When you take the container out, run warm water over it to loosen the ice from the sides.
■ Before sliding the puppet out, poke the skirt over the wooden stick so it is resting at the base of the puppet face.
■ Add several petticoats of paper towel to protect your hand from the cold.
■ With your hand under the skirt, hold onto the wooden stick and turn the puppet over. Pull the container off and get ready to perform! (See illustration 3.)

Banana Bonanza

For a cool treat, peel a banana, wrap it in foil, and place it in the freezer for a couple of hours.

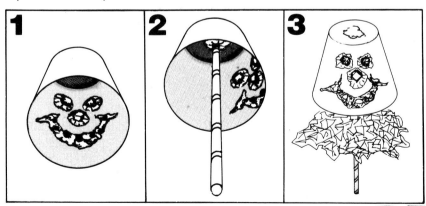

Cold Stuff

COOL CUBES

Make up some ice cubes with class for your long, cold drinks.

You'll Need:

Ice cube tray
Fruit pieces (*Berries, melon balls, and orange slices work well.*)
Water or fruit juice

Here's How:

■ Drop the fruit pieces into each section of the ice cube tray.
■ Fill the tray with water or juice and freeze.
■ Add the cubes to cold drinks for a tasty treat.

Kitchen Challenge 4.

How can you make an ice cube somersault?

See page 32
for the answer.

Ice Cream Magic

Nothing beats ice cream for a cool and frosty snack.
Try out these recipes for ice cream with pizzazz.

ICE CREAM CUPS

Make a cup of good old-fashioned soft ice cream, using salt and ice!

You'll Need:

1 1/2 cups crushed ice
1/2 cup salt
1/2 cup whipping cream
1/4 cup sugar
1/4 tsp vanilla
Small paper cup
Styrofoam cup (large enough for the paper one to fit inside)
Wooden ice cream stick
Plastic wrap
Rubber band

Here's How:

■ Mix the cream, vanilla, and sugar together in the paper cup.
■ Use the rubber band to fasten the plastic wrap in place over the paper cup.
■ Mix the salt and ice together in the styrofoam cup.
■ Place the paper cup into the bigger cup so that the ice and salt mixture surrounds it.
■ Now remove the plastic wrap. Be careful not to get any salty ice into your ice cream.
■ Stir the cream mixture off and on for the next 15 to 20 minutes. By then you'll have delicious soft ice cream to taste!

Pass the Spoons

In 1985 the largest ice cream sundae ever to be made was served up at the Disneyland Hotel in Anaheim, California. Want to beat this record? You'd have to gather together enough ice cream to almost equal the weight of 2 elephants, add just over 25 bathtubs of topping and end with 15 pails of whipping cream!

Cold Stuff

WONDERFUL WATERMELON

This watermelon wasn't grown on a vine—it's made of ice cream! Make it in the morning and eat it for dessert at dinnertime.

You'll Need:

4 cups green ice cream
4 cups pink ice cream
1/2 cup chocolate chips
Large bowl lined with tinfoil
Spoon
Alarm clock (*Set the alarm for the times mentioned.*)
Platter

Here's How:

■ Chill the bowl for 30 minutes in the freezer.
■ Shape a layer of green ice cream around the inside of the bowl to a depth of your thumb.
■ Put the bowl back in the freezer.
■ After 3 hours, start softening the pink ice cream until you can stir in the chocolate chips. Spoon the mixture into the bowl. Freeze until firm, about 3 more hours.
■ When it's time for dessert, turn the bowl upside down on a plate and remove bowl and foil. Mmmmmmmmm!

Crazy Cans

Collect cans of all shapes and sizes.
Then make the games you see here
and have a crazy can afternoon of fun.

STRUTTING ON STILTS

Walk tall on a pair of juice cans.

You'll Need:

2 large, empty juice cans with a hole punched on each side near the top (*Ask an adult to make these holes with a hammer and nail.*)

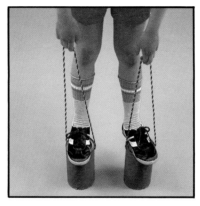

2 pieces of rope (long enough to loop through the holes and up to your hands when you stand on the cans)

Here's How:

■ Thread the rope through the holes in each can.
■ Tie a knot so that you can hold the rope in your hands comfortably when you stand on the cans.
■ Now pull the ropes tight and away you strut!

TELEPHONE TALK

Believe it or not, you can talk to a friend through a tin can!

You'll Need:

2 tin cans with holes punched in the bottom (*Ask an adult to help you use a hammer and nail to make the holes.*)
Piece of long string
Buttons

Fun and Games

GOOFY GOLF

Make an indoor golf game — great fun for a rainy day!

You'll Need:

5 cleaned-out tin cans of different
    sizes
Paper clips
Construction paper
Wooden ice cream sticks
White glue
Markers
Small ball
Club (baseball bat, broom,
    golf club)

Here's How:

■ Put the cans in order from the
largest to the smallest with the
open ends facing out.

■ Cut out squares of paper and
paste on the ends of wooden
sticks. Glue the other end of each
stick to a can.
■ Give the largest can the score
of 2 and work up to 10 for the
smallest one.
■ Clip the cans together tightly
with paper clips.
■ Now practice putting with the
ball and club. What is *your* best
score?

Clank, clank!

**Imagine it...North
America throws out 40
billion pop cans in
total each year. On
average, that's about
150 cans per person.
So, the next time you
finish a pop, think
before you throw. Is
there another use for
the can? Is there a
recycling depot
nearby? Who wants a
world knee-deep in
cans instead of grass
and trees?**

Here's How:

■ Thread the string through the
holes.

■ Add a button on each end of
the string before you tie a knot
there.
■ Keep one can and give the
other to a friend.
■ Pull the string taut and then
whisper into the can to your
friend.

Fantastic Faces

Make a fabulous face.
Will it be a frightening flashlight face?
Or a funny face sandwich to eat? Or both?

FLASHLIGHT FACES

Take an egg or some muffin ingredients, find a flashlight, and make a spooky mask for Halloween.

You'll Need:

Egg Faces:
Egg white in a cup
Eggshell broken in tiny bits or
    strips of tissue
Hair drier
Flashlight
Glitter, make-up (optional)

Muffin Face:
Honey
Bran cereal
Corn meal
Water-based paints
Orange peel teeth
Flashlight

Here's How:

Egg Faces:

■ Smear the egg white on your face.
■ Stick the eggshell bits or tissue strips to it, and then smear more egg white over the shell bits or the ends of the strips.

■ Dry the egg white with the hair drier.
■ Hold a flashlight under your chin in a dark room and look in the mirror. **Yucko!**

Muffin Face:

■ Spread honey over your face, except around your eyes.
■ Stick the corn meal and bran to the honey.
■ Paint on eyebrows.
■ Pop in your orange peel teeth, and put a flashlight under your chin. **Aaaaaah!**

What is the longest word?

Smiles (a mile between 2 S's)! And did you know that human beings are the only creatures in the world who smile when they're happy?

FUNNY FACES

Invite your friends over to make their very own funny face sandwiches for lunch.

You'll Need:

Bread slices
Peanut butter or cheese spread
Eyes (radish slices, grape halves,
    cherry tomatoes,
    blueberries…)
Noses (carrot sticks, cucumber
    slices, cheese chunks…)
Smiles (avocado slices, apple
    eighths, orange pieces…)
Hair (bean sprouts, celery leaves,
    watercress leaves…)
Knives
Plates

Here's How:

■ Before your friends arrive, ask an adult to help you slice up the fruits and vegetables for face decorations.
■ Assemble the pieces on a platter.
■ Put out the bread and spreads.
■ Then let your friends start creating!

Fun and Games

Pick the Pairs

**Make some play clay markers
and have a game of "Pick the Pairs."**

You'll Need:

2 cups flour
1/2 cup salt
1 cup water
Mixing bowl, measuring cup,
    cookie tray
Rolling pin
Cutter (*A film tube or top of baby
    bottle or small jar works well.*)
Pencil
Poster paint, acrylic paint, or
    magic markers
Paintbrushes
Clear nail polish

Here's How:

■ Mix the first three ingredients
together.
■ Roll out the play clay on a
smooth floured surface with a
rolling pin.

■ Make at least 30 round shapes
with the cutter. (A few extras may
be useful if you spoil any in the
next step.) They should be uniform
in size and appearance.
■ Create 15 pairs of markers by
making a different design on each
pair with a sharp pencil.
■ Let the markers sit on a cookie
tray overnight to dry.
■ The next day ask an adult to
heat the oven to 300°F. Bake the
markers for an hour.
■ After they have cooled, paint
them with bright colors.
■ For shiny markers, coat with
clear nail polish after paint is fully
dry.

**Kitchen
Challenge**
5.

**How can you give
away part of yourself,
but still keep it?**

**See page 32
for the answer.**

HOW TO PLAY

■ Place all the markers upside
down.
■ Turn them over two at a time
and look at the patterns. Do you
see a pair?
■ If yes, remove the pair from the
game. If no, turn the pieces upside
down and let a friend take a turn.
■ If you are playing by yourself,
try again. How long will it take
you to find all the pairs?

****If you are a checker fan,
paint nine markers black and
nine markers red.**

****If you like playing "Fish,"
double the recipe, and make
15 sets of markers, four with
the same pattern in each set.**

**Here are
some patterns
you might put
on your
markers.**

**What other
ones can you
think of?**

**Can you match up
the 11 pairs here?**

Fun and Games

Answers

Kitchen Challenge 1.

To see a chicken bone bend, place it in a glass of vinegar for a few days. The acid in the vinegar slowly eats away the hard calcium in the bone. A small leg bone takes about 5 days to go rubbery.

Kitchen Challenge 2.

All you have to do is roll the paper into a tube (about one thumb across) and tape! This makes the paper strong, rigid and round. The roundness ensures that the weight of the cookbook is evenly distributed when you place the book on top of the tube.

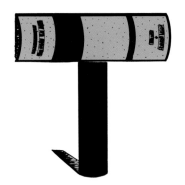

Kitchen Challenge 3.

When iodine is dropped on a food that contains starch, it turns black, and pretzels contain starch. Starch is a chain of simple sugars stored in plants, and it is one of the elements in food that gives you energy. What other foods in your kitchen contain starch? *WARNING: Do not eat any food tested with iodine; it is poisonous.*

Kitchen Challenge 4.

Place the ice cube in a dish of hot water and watch it flip—over and over and over!

Kitchen Challenge 5.

Use play clay and plaster of paris to make a foot or hand mold.

Here's How:

■ Make up a batch of the play clay recipe.
■ Pat out a pattie the size of your foot or hand to a depth of half a thumb.
■ Press your hand or foot into the play clay gently. Don't make a hole in the bottom!
■ Coat the indentation well with lots of cooking oil.
■ Mix up plaster of paris with water until it is the consistency of thick cream.
■ Pour this mixture into your body mold.
■ Let it sit overnight and then peel away the play clay. Be careful when peeling around the fingers.
■ Decorate, and give yourself away as a paperweight!